"Can you hear me?" Beth whispered, her cheeks turning red. She tried again, a bit louder. "Hello? I hear you talking. Is anyone there?"

The song continued without even a pause. Beth scrubbed her fingers through her hair, then got as close to shouting as she dared in the closed space with people right outside the door.

"Either tell me what you want or leave me alone!"

The voices stopped.

Beth tried to hold perfectly still, not sure if she wanted an answer or for the whole thing to be over. She could probably adjust to not having music anymore, but not to the constant noise.

The low, empty circuit hum in her ears intensified, and a voice floated up like a distant station on her great-uncle's old tube radio.

"Been wonderin' if anyone was there." The woman spoke with a thick dialect that was hard to understand, but Beth thought it had to be from close by. "Been tryin' to get through for a powerful long time."

Beth opened her mouth twice before any words made it out.

Songs in the Mountain: Book One of the Voices through Time Series

Copyright © 2016 by Kari A. Kilgore

All rights reserved

Published 2016 by Spiral Publishing, Ltd. www.spiralpublishing.net

Book and cover design copyright © 2016 by Spiral Publishing, Ltd.

Cover art copyright © 2016 by Kari A. Kilgore

ISBN-13: 978-0-9908875-4-6

Library of Congress Control Number: 2016917644

For Jason
The best traveling companion I ever could have hoped for.

SONGS IN THE MOUNTAIN

BOOK ONE OF THE VOICES THROUGH TIME SERIES

KARI KILGORE

SPIRAL PUBLISHING, LTD.

Chapter 1

Beth Azen leaned back in the squeaky office chair, rubbing her burning eyes. The desk itself wasn't much more than a countertop wedged in between overcrowded shelves and rows of filing cabinets. The town hall's scanner was old enough to give off a sharp, hot plastic smell after a couple of hours.

She'd worked in more than one musty archives room over twenty years as a writer, but this one in her native Hartstown, Virginia, had to be the most compact. Access to over a century of Boun County's history was worth a bit of discomfort.

Worse than her sinus rebellion against the aromatic space, Beth's fingertips were raw from handing dozens of glass plate negatives. The plates were a bit larger than a paperback and about a quarter of an inch thick, but heavier than they looked. The greenish edges were straight but wavy, like they'd been melted out instead of cut. Even through the sweaty blue gloves, she felt like she'd been rubbing sandpaper all day long.

Her nerves were just as frazzled. Beth wasn't sure if it

would be worse to break one of the negatives, break the glass of the scanner trying to place one of them, or cut herself with who knows what had been on the razor-sharp edges for over a hundred years.

Most of the negatives didn't look like much, with one side smooth and the other rough with varying shades of black and gray. The images Beth extracted from the persnickety things were gorgeous, though, more sharp and clear than almost any other medium. Photographers willing to lug chunks of glass though the mountains back then had her full respect.

Beth wondered if the to-be-scanned pile would ever be smaller than the finished stack in the box beside her on the gray carpeted floor. She always got to this point in a long project, when she felt like she was never going to get to the end. Knowing she'd get over that helpless feeling eventually didn't make any difference. Beth took a sip of cold coffee, at least two cups past too much, and got back to work, taking out another of the delicate slides.

The town manager didn't want anyone to bring in music or even use earbuds like most places did, but Beth didn't mind. She constantly had a song in her head, from the time she woke up until she fell asleep, and probably all night long, too. She'd heard it described as some kind of brain disorder on the radio a while back, but that didn't make sense to her. She couldn't imagine how bored people got if they didn't have something to listen to.

She lined the rectangular piece of glass up against the side of the scanner, put a blank sheet of paper over it, and lowered a huge square light to a couple of inches above everything. The lamp was bigger than what her dentist used, and the heat added to the closed in feeling in the tiny room. Nothing else she'd tried would bring out the old images.

Putting together a massive book of images with the town

historical society wasn't one of Beth's typical non-fiction writing projects, but she enjoyed her side trips into book design and publishing. Her parents and her hound mutt Janie certainly appreciated her staying home for a few months instead of traveling for research. And she enjoyed the chance to wear her most comfortable faded jeans, old flannel shirts, and sneakers without asking about anybody's dress code. She flipped through the other photos on her screen while the scanner whined and clicked.

This corner in the Virginia coalfields struggled even now, but the poverty a hundred years ago was horrifying. The rudimentary houses and muddy roads didn't bother Beth nearly as much as the faces of the men, women, and children.

So many of them seemed much older than they could have been, understandable with a hard way of life and dangerous work logging or coal mining. The kids in particular looked as old as the photographs. Seeing that era coming to an end didn't disturb Beth at all.

A chirpy Minnesota-nice voice from right behind her did.

"Hey Beth! How's it goin' today?"

"Doing fine, Tina. You?"

"Great! Just checkin' to see if you need anything."

Tina had moved with her husband a year ago when he started teaching at the new optometry school in town, and she clearly loved everything about the change of pace from northern city life. Beth appreciated the interest, especially compared to being isolated in a cold, dank basement like she'd been on past jobs, but sometimes Tina was a little too eager to help. And today her strong, flowery perfume was one too many aromas in the tiny space.

"I'm good, thank you," Beth said.

"Just let me know, then."

Tina grinned and spun on her heel, her long blonde hair

and pink gauze skirt throwing up a bit more of that thick aroma. Beth tasted the scent on the back of her throat, even over the strong coffee, and her head was swimming. She rubbed her temples, trying to fend off a headache. When the scanner clicked again and stopped, Beth froze.

Chapter 2

SILENCE. Not only the lack of grinding mechanical noise, but complete silence. For the first time since she'd been old enough to notice, her own mind was eerily quiet. Beth shook her head. She heard her short brown hair shifting, the low voices of other people in the conference room behind her, the tick of the cooling scanner, but nothing else. She even heard her own heart beating faster with every second.

Beth pulled off the gloves and grabbed her jacket, then darted out the side door before Tina or anyone else could stop her. She had to get some fresh air, even if it was well below freezing. She'd been working too long, as usual. Being stuck in a closet-sized room full of dusty and moldy boxes was getting to her.

She leaned against the red brick building, staring past the fire hall next door at the gray mountains dotted with dark green pine trees soaring all around the town. The only sounds in this sheltered alley were a few cars passing on the street and tree limbs creaking in the bitterly cold wind. Her hearing was fine, even sharper than normal.

In fact, Beth heard a low hum now, like an amplifier

turned up too loud. That had almost drowned out the music before, but only when she was too tired or getting sick. Maybe it was time to knock off for the day. One of the best parts of freelancing in her hometown for a change was being able to go home at three if she needed to.

As she got closer to the archives room back inside, meaning to put everything away, shut down, and get out of there, Beth slowed. She turned her head from side to side, trying to figure out where the sound was coming from. A woman's voice, low and sorrowful, getting louder with every step she took. That didn't make sense with the strict policy about radios or music players, but Beth heard it all the same.

She glanced around the empty meeting room. All the office doors were closed and the metal folding chairs were stacked up against the walls. Beth shook her head and stepped into the archives room.

The voice split into many, all singing a dirge Beth had never heard before. She didn't recognize the language either. Some sort of European, maybe, hard to place. She pulled her phone out of her pocket, but it was set to silent. The computer didn't have speakers, and she didn't see any kind of intercom.

The singing shifted to an old-time funeral, clear even without hearing the words.

"That's enough for you today," Beth said under her breath. She picked up the last negative she'd scanned without bothering with the gloves, not worried about fingerprints for the moment.

Beth almost dropped the piece of glass when the singing got much louder. She carefully put it back down, and the noise level decreased. Beth raised the huge scanning lamp and held the image under it. A group of people sat and stood on a small hillside, all staring solemnly at the unseen camera. Long gowns for women and dark suits for men, hair in braids or buns, and elaborate hats, all from around the turn of the last century. Exactly like all the other photos she'd seen over the past few weeks. The freshly filled grave in the middle explained why everyone wore their Sunday best.

The singing died down for a few seconds, then they launched into one Beth did recognize. "Rock of Ages," but the words were oddly accented, hard to pick out. She caught herself trying to figure out where the singers had come from. The nationality of the mourners was the least of Beth's problems.

She packed up and shut down, relieved when putting the slide in the box on the floor muffled the singing. Beth would have felt a lot better if it had stopped altogether. She tapped her fingernails on the metal doorframe, contemplating asking Tina if she heard anything. Trying to imagine the response whichever way it went put an end to that idea. Beth closed the door and walked away slowly, the song getting fainter with every step. Even when she got in her car and turned on her own music, the strange voices never did disappear.

Chapter 3

Two days later, Beth was feeling more rough and sharp around the edges, just like those chunks of greenish glass, than she wanted to admit. The singing had only gotten louder, and now she heard people talking low and soft in between the songs. The sensation that she'd be able to make out the words if she only tried a little bit harder felt like grit inside her brain.

Walking into the archives room at the town hall made it worse. Handling the slides was almost deafening, but at least the music changed depending on what she was looking at. Sprightly, joyful fiddles, funeral dirges and hymns, schoolhouse learning chants, and even a bit of early bluegrass. Beth could change the tunes with different slides almost like a radio.

None of the other archived materials, whether postcards, printed photos, or newer plastic negatives, had an effect. Only the pieces of glass. The constant undercurrent was as maddening as her own music had been comforting.

Rather than go across the street for lunch, Beth got a fresh notebook and closed the door. No matter how stuffy it got, the last thing she needed was Tina or anyone else wandering in while she was talking to herself. She pulled out the funeral picture, the one that started all this strangeness. Murmuring voices replaced the singing, but she couldn't quite make out any words. A few more songs went by with no more success.

"Can you hear me?" she whispered, her cheeks turning red. She tried again, a bit louder. "Hello? I hear you talking. Is anyone there?"

The song continued without even a pause. Beth scrubbed her fingers through her hair, then got as close to shouting as she dared in the closed space with people right outside the door.

"Either tell me what you want or leave me alone!"

The voices stopped.

Beth tried to hold perfectly still, not sure if she wanted an answer or for the whole thing to be over. She could probably adjust to not having music anymore, but not to the constant noise.

The low, empty circuit hum in her ears intensified, and a voice floated up like a distant station on her great-uncle's old tube radio.

"Been wonderin' if anyone was there." The woman spoke with a thick dialect that was hard to understand, but Beth thought it had to be from close by. "Been tryin' to get through for a powerful long time."

Beth opened her mouth twice before any words made it out.

"Trying to get through from where?"

"Well, from right here," the woman said. It sounded like rii-chyer. "Bountyfield. Ain't that where you are?"

"This is Hartstown, but I'm in Boun County," Beth said, leaning over to grab the computer mouse. She followed a hunch and scrolled through the manuscript file to the section about county origins. "This used to be called Bountyfield a long time ago, so I guess that's where I am."

"Well then, you aready know what I want."

Beth let out a short laugh, shaking her head. The list of what she knew sat pretty much at zero.

"No, ma'am. I'm afraid I don't know anything. Maybe we can start with why on earth I can hear you at all?"

"That question only you can answer. I been called a wise woman, a seer, sometimes even a witch, among my people. You anything like that?"

Beth shook herself and sat forward, scribbling as much as she remembered about the conversation so far. If nothing else, she wanted a record of such a vivid break from reality. Assuming she recovered, this would make a great story someday.

"I don't think anyone's ever called me wise," she said, smiling. "Not even close."

"It don't have to be you, now. If you hear me at all, some of your folks had an ear for such."

Beth tapped the pen on the nearly full page, trying to imagine what this mystery woman meant. Her concerns about having some kind of breakdown led her to the answer.

"I had, well, not exactly a wise woman," she said. "One of my great-grandmothers was supposed to have a little trouble with reality. I don't remember her very well."

Beth stopped, chills running down her arms and legs. Granny Johnson hadn't just had trouble. She'd heard voices. Voices no one else could hear. When the woman spoke again, Beth jumped hard enough to leave a mark on the page.

"Reality depends a lot on who's seein' it and who's callin' it, you ask me. What's your name? If we're gonna talk like this and get anything done, I need to know who I'm talkin' with."

"I'm Beth. Beth Azen. I guess I should have asked sooner,

but what's your name? And what do you mean, get anything done?"

"I'm Clina Jane. What I mean is fix this pizen down deep in our mountains. I reckon more than enough lives been lost to it, certainly from where you're sittin'."

Chapter 4

BETH KNEW what Clina meant by pizen, but she hadn't heard it for a long, long time. She thought that dialect had just about died out around the time her family's reunions stopped. Her mind seemed to focus on the strangest of details today. A disembodied voice was telling her about poison in the mountains, and she was worried about the pronunciation?

"I'm glad to meet you, Clina, but I don't understand any of this. What poison? You mean the water?"

"Same as before, you got to tell me. Could be in water by now, sure. Do a lot of folks still die right around there, Beth? More than you can count for?"

For the first time since she'd heard the strange singing in her head, Beth wasn't confused. Digging into this book project showed her all too clearly how many mine disasters were in the county's past, with quite a few killed in timber and railroad operations as well. It did seem far too many for such a small town.

"Well, yeah, I suppose they do." Beth's mind kept searching through her internal files, more crowded but better organized than the tiny room she was in. A lot of people died in automotive accidents close by, too. And she knew of more drownings than made sense with the small number of creeks and one river. "I hadn't really thought about it, but Hartstown seems to be unlucky in a lot of ways."

"Unlucky may have been the trouble way back at the start, but things have gone a ways past luck by now. A bad wrong's been lodged down under the ground here, one that has to be made right. I been tryin' to get through to someone on your side for so long I like to give up. Now that I found you, Beth, we got to get busy."

"Hang on, I'm not even sure this is real," Beth said. "Any of this. Even if I had any reason to believe you, why would I believe some poison was down in the mountains causing trouble?"

"Look around and answer that second part for yourself," Clina said, her voice sharp and testy. "Might be able to help with the first part, though. Why'd you hear me in the first place?"

"Why... How the hell should I know?"

"Good girl, good girl." Beth was sure she heard chuckling in her mind, raspy and satisfied. "Got some backbone after all. Jes tell me what you was doing when it started."

"I was scanning these old slides," Beth said, wishing she had something to scowl at. "Old photographs, pictures."

"Now you're on to it. Like as not I'm in one of those pitchurs."

"Well, it's a whole group of people. We couldn't find any names for this one."

"That don't matter. Listen to me, now. We never did pitchurs less it was something big like a wedding or a funeral, maybe a baptizin'. What kind you got there?"

"A funeral," Beth said, her heart pounding. "For a coal miner."

"Makes sense. That's who we mostly had em for, and way too many a those. Can you tell the name on the stone?"

Beth picked up the slide in shaking hands, making sure she had a firm grip on the sharp edges. This was one of the batch the historical society had rescued from someone's basement. The years of damp hadn't done the glass any favors.

"I'm sorry, that part's too dirty and smudged."

"Then why don't you clean it?" Clina sounded like she was talking to a small child. "What's the point of having a thing if you leave it too dirty to use?"

Beth snorted, feeling like her mother was lecturing her about keeping her room clean. The reason she'd accepted a few weeks ago when starting research for the book sounded pitifully thin to her ears. Some part of her knew Clina wouldn't be happy with her explanation.

"For these I'm not supposed to. We have to leave the slides as they are so they won't get damaged any further."

"I never heered of such nonsense. If you're wantin' some kind of proof, you just have to get you some soap and break that little rule right now."

Beth sat back in her chair, shaking her head. She didn't want to lose access to the archives, but not doing simple cleaning had been driving her crazy. Probably not as crazy as never figuring out what was going on inside her own head would.

"Okay, Clina. I can't use soap on these," Beth said, laughing at the surreal argument. "Hang on, I've got some water right here."

She picked up her water bottle and pulled out one of the tissues she always carried in such a dusty environment. Turning the slide over first to make sure she had the smooth side, not the coated side that held the photo, Beth tilted the bottle into the tissue for a second. She rubbed the slide in a circle big enough to include the tombstone, trying to make the edges uneven enough to look natural.

"I see…looks like Fekete."

Clina was silent long enough that Beth started to wonder if the whole strange episode was over. Maybe she'd backed the delusion into a corner asking for proof she could only provide with her own eyes. She was glad she'd put the slide down when the voice spoke.

"That'd be Gez Fekete, died in 1908. I know the very pitchur you have there. Look to the left side of his stone, where the trees are, then count three people from the end. You're lookin' at Clina Jane wearin' my finest."

Beth leaned closer, then turned to the computer. She found the image in a few seconds and zoomed in on the mourners more than her eyes ever could have. The women and children stood together in a group behind dark-suited men. The third one in was a slender woman wearing a long white dress with a dark belt, standing with one hand on her hip. Beth saw pale skin and dark hair under a huge, white hat.

"I see you just fine, but that doesn't really prove anything," Beth said, feeling a little guilty, even if she was talking to herself. "I can see this for myself."

"Sounds to me like I did good when I got through to you, Beth. You might have enough smarts to get this thang done. Tell you what, go look in whatever records you got there under Gez Fekete. He was from way off over the ocean, Hungary, I think. Even printed his last name before his first like they did over there. He married a girl from Bountyfield, and his five kids was born here. The last 'un just a few weeks before he met his end under the ground. You'll find his missus changed their name over to Black once he was gone."

"Records," Beth said to herself, closing her eyes. "They have census records next door at the courthouse, marriage records too. Anything else you think I'll find while we're at this?"

"Now I don't mind one little bit that you don't believe me. That's why you're the right one for a tough job like this. Go on and look up a thang or two on me, then."

Beth leaned forward and wrote the dates, names, and places Clina gave her. She didn't know whether verifying everything would make her feel better or worse.

"I'll go check this out." Beth put all the equipment on standby and picked up her bag and jacket. "I'm assuming I'll still be able to hear you over there, so you'll know how it's going."

"You have right many questions only you can answer. Seems to me you can hear me best when you're with those pitchurs, but I reckon we'll find out."

Chapter 5

BETH WALKED BACK into the archives room two hours later, nose running terribly from the midewy records room at the courthouse. The floodwaters from a hundred years ago might never have receded by the way the huge old record books destroyed her sinuses. Under her discomfort, she was dazed and more than a little afraid.

"Clina? I'm back. Can you hear me better?"

"Clear as a bell, Beth. Find that proof you was lookin' for?"

Beth sat down hard in the creaky old chair, not sure how to answer. She picked up the glass image of the long ago funeral scene, her fingertip touching Clina's white hat. Might as well start talking.

"Everything you said checked out, down to the dates when they had them. I don't understand how or why, but you're telling me the truth. How do you remember things so clearly?"

"It's the only way I know to remember. I kindly think I'm still back here, when all this is going on. At least some part of me is. Reckon we can work together and clear out that pizen I told you about?"

Beth laughed louder than she meant to, but it felt too good to stop. At least until she started sneezing out the mildew. Five in a row took care of most of it, not very neatly.

"And exactly how do you propose we do that?" she said, trying to catch her breath. "I still don't know what poison you're talking about."

"Now that you decided to believe in me, maybe you'll believe in this. Thar's a tiny little mine pit, operated before I was born, and all the big ones around it claimed many a life. More than their fair share, some say. The trouble all goes right back to one of the first men to go under the ground after coal for his house. First one to die, too."

"What happened to him?"

"Rock fall far as I know, same as killed more than's ever been counted. The way it happened ain't the problem. Fact is this man was so far off away from home when he passed. His bones rest there still, deep in that pit where he died."

Beth rubbed her arms, trying to soothe the hairs standing on end. Her grandfather had spoken of going down in the mine and never knowing if even his bones would make the trip back up. No one knew for certain how many met that fate long before anyone kept good records.

"That happened a lot, certainly with all the disasters here," she said. "How could one man make the land poison?"

"That one man came from across the water, too, a place where the dead was buried together back to the beginning of time. Great, long graves, where even poor folk was kept from being alone after they drew their last."

"How can you possibly know this, Clina?"

Beth didn't want to say it, but she couldn't imagine the education of a woman born in these mountains so long ago went far enough to cover burial mounds in Britain and Europe.

"I hear him is how. He's been singing, crying his lonesome heart out for all this time. Folks still livin' and breathin' catch his song in their bones, on the backs of their necks, in the goose walkin' over their graves. Once you pass on like I have, you hear his cry so loud and clear you can't ignore it no more."

"What's he crying for?" Beth whispered.

"I reckon what he wants is company. And he's done all he can to make that happen. I know a touch from when my husband died years before I did. A body so lonesome pulls others to him any way he can. Out of the rock, out of the air, out of the water. That's the pizen that's filled this land full of so much blood and sorrow."

Beth jumped so hard she grunted when someone knocked on the metal door. Damn, she'd forgotten to close it when she came back in. She knew her face was bright red before she turned around, but there was no help for it.

"Hi Beth, how's it goin'?"

"I'm just fine, Tina. You startled me is all."

"I'm sorry!" Tina said, putting a ring-laden hand over her heart. "I just wanted to remind you we're closin' a little early for the community forum. You can stay as long as you like, but it's gonna be noisy. Big crowd tonight."

Something tickled at the back of Beth's mind. An alert from her investigator's instinct that she knew better than to ignore, but she couldn't catch it.

"Great, thanks for the warning."

When Tina walked away, Beth finally heard people gathering in the conference room. Chatter and movement were loud in the normally quiet space.

"Sorry, Clina. I think we might be done for the night," she said, keeping her voice low. "I can't sit in here and talk to myself with the whole town outside the door. Half of them thought I was crazy for going away to college and again every time I leave to work on a story. The other half think I'm crazy for coming back."

"Sounds to me like you hit it just about right. You in a hurry to get home to your own man?"

"Not at the moment," Beth said. She didn't want to respond the same way she did when some of her relatives asked about her single status over and over again. "Just me and my dog."

"Dog's company, but you should have you someone to talk to in the middle of the night. That's some powerful lonely time."

"You're right." Beth started to put the slide back in the protective box, then paused. "Listen, I'm still not sure what you think I can do for this miner. I don't even know where to start. How could I possibly find him?"

"I might could point you in the right direction, then I reckon it's up to you," Clina said. "You'd likely find him easier than you think. This thing in your head that lets you hear me might not be so easy to turn off. It might well work for him and a bunch more folks besides."

"Perfect. That's just what I need," Beth said as she shut everything down. "A bunch of grouchy oldtimers carrying on inside my mind all the time."

"Might find you learn a thang or two," Clina said, and Beth was sure she heard laughter. "No way to know til we get there."

Chapter 6

Beth closed the door behind her before she got a look at
the room. Almost all the metal chairs facing her were filled,
and a thousand people seemed to be staring. Clammy sweat
covered her body in an instant. She tried to smile, then
walked as fast as she could toward the exit.

Just as she reached the door, she glanced back over her
shoulder. The stack of brochures on the long table beside her
set her inner alarm off again. The state department of land
reclamation's information about…old abandoned mines.

Beth didn't much believe in coincidences, especially not
this big. She turned around and took a seat near the back.
Clina and what sounded like a hundred of her friends were
singing hymns again, soft and low in her head.

Over an hour later, Beth stood in the corner while it
seemed like everyone else in town lined up to ask questions.
The presenter did his best not to look at his watch, but he
clearly had somewhere else to be. Beth willed him to wait
just a few more minutes. When the last person finally headed
out, she walked up to the front.

"Listen, I'm sorry to bother you," she said, holding out

her hand. "I won't take long. I'm Beth Azen. I know you need to get out of here, but I might be able to help you get the word out about this project."

"Good to meet you, Beth," he said. His grip was warm and firm. "Mark Hersch. Any ideas you have would be great, but I'm afraid they want to close up here."

"Well, no, we can wait a while longer," Tina said from a few feet behind Beth. She was smiling, but she glanced at her husband and two little boys out in the hall. The kids were as blond, blue-eyed, and pale as their parents, but they spoke as if they'd lived in Hartstown all their lives. "Beth would be a great contact for ya, Mr. Hersch. She's a reporter and a writer."

"Maybe we should talk then," Mark said, his bright green eyes lighting up with his smile. He was just over Beth's height of five-eleven, and he seemed to be in his mid-thirties too. "It's so hard to get through to small landowners when we only have rumors about where some of these old mines were located."

"Oh, she's just perfect, then!" Tina said, beaming. "Beth's been here for a few weeks workin' on a history book about Boun County."

"That's what gave me the idea," Beth said. She hoped the strange turn her project had taken didn't show on her face. "If you haven't had dinner yet, we can walk over to Rayburn's."

"Sure, I'd like to hear more," he said, then turned to Tina. "Thank you again for the room, ma'am."

As Tina locked up behind them, the boys ran screaming into the once again empty space. Beth was still a bit in shock over basically asking a man out to dinner, one she'd never laid eyes on before tonight. At least he was easy on the eyes.

"Just as well we got out of there before those kids exploded," she said as they walked across the street in the harsh wind, only having to wait for a couple of cars at just after seven. "When did you start focusing on these smaller mines?"

"We're still working on several big ones, but a lot of the stream runoff in Boun County seems to be coming from these old, unpermitted mines. No one really kept records for a long time. Once they did, a bunch of the smaller ones were already abandoned. Cleaning up these little mines has been a pet project of mine for a while. Finally starting to happen."

Beth's mind worked at top speed as they got settled in the Italian-themed restaurant. Murals of Roman statues and ancient city vistas contrasted with the red vinyl booths and college basketball game muted on two flat-screen TVs hanging from the ceiling. The food here was hardly gourmet, but it was good. Her stomach growled at the rich, yeasty smell of pizza and frying potatoes.

She tried to think of all the reasons he'd turn her crazy idea down. If Beth managed this, she might solve more than Clina's problems.

Chapter 7

"So what's your idea to help out?" Mark said, pulling off his blue state jacket and running his hands through his unruly strawberry blond hair. He was dressed as casually as she was once he shed the official uniform, with blue jeans and a faded burgundy Virginia Tech t-shirt. "And tell me more about your book."

"Those two kind of go together," Beth said, taking a drink of her Coke to buy a bit more time. This had to be good. "A couple of days ago, I was scanning a pitch…a picture of a coal miner's funeral from the turn of the last century. I remembered reading about how they sometimes didn't have anything to bury, especially with a rock fall or a bad explosion. I'm sorry to be morbid, but do you come across anything like that when you're re-mining?"

"Now there's a different sort of question," he said, blinking. "As a matter of fact, we've come across bones that are clearly human a few times, especially in these pre-regulation mines. Strange as it sounds, that's part of what got me into this line of work. When I was fifteen, I found a leg bone in an abandoned house coal pit I never should have been inside of. Were you thinking of writing about that?"

"Kind of. What do you do with those remains?"

"So far we've just been storing them unless we can identify anyone who was killed in that specific mine. A bunch of them are unclaimed." He sat forward, his expression more curious than confused.

"Well, something else I'm writing about for this book is the cemetery in town," Beth said. "It's not far from right here. It's pretty amazing, really. The markers are in almost a dozen different languages. Most people don't realize how many immigrants came here to work in the mines back then. There's also a mass grave they used after a couple of the big disasters."

Beth watched Mark's eyes, hoping he would put the rest together for himself. Clina's singing inside her head kept her calm instead of putting her on edge for the first time. If she could get this to work out, and if Clina's hunch about Beth being able to hear more than one voice was true, the mystery miner might have his community resting place after all. Mark rubbed his neatly trimmed reddish beard, then nodded.

"You know, that's not a bad idea," he said slowly. "I have family in the town cemetery, but I didn't know about the mass grave. If we put the bones there and you write about it, we could create some sympathy and good publicity for our program and for your book."

"We could, but I was thinking we could do something sooner to get people involved with what you're doing." Beth sat back as the waiter delivered a gorgeous pepperoni pizza. She wanted to dig in, partly to quiet her constantly rumbling stomach. Partly to put this off, even if she did scorch her mouth. "How about if we go into one of the mines that's rumored to have bodies inside, see if we find one, and write about it?"

"You are optimistic!" Mark said with a grin, sliding two steaming slices onto her plate before doing the same for himself. "That would be great, but you have better connections than I do if you can find a long-lost miner on the first few tries."

Beth laughed, trying not to let it get away from her. If he only knew…

"I've been through a lot of records lately," she said. "And I'm a pretty good investigator. I've tracked down things far less likely than this. Think we could give it a try?"

Mark took a bite and hissed cool air over his tongue. He shrugged.

"I'd have to pull some serious strings to get you in on one of these jobs. We want to take care of these runoff spots, but the other thing is these old mines are dangerous. Rotten timber, no roof support, definitely no ventilation fans."

"How about this, then," Beth said, encouraged that he hadn't said no. "I'll pull my research together and ask around a little. If I find a likely spot, I'd bet the possibility of finding someone will get you access to the land. Then if you do find something, go ahead and shore things up. Make it safer. Right before you're ready to seal the mine, I go in, take pictures, and we get the bones. I promise you that story will get you access to a whole lot more land."

Beth took a bite of her cooler and absolutely delicious pizza, the crispy crust, soft cheese, and sharp pepperoni seeming like the best thing she'd ever tasted right then. Either Mark would like the idea, or he wouldn't. There were plenty of obstacles, assuming she could even hear another voice besides Clina's, not to mention the safety issues. But if he wasn't interested, she was stopped cold before she even got started.

"That may just be too good to pass up," he said, nodding and staring into space. "We don't go in expecting to get coal out of most of these individual mines, so no worries about antsy operators hoping to get their investment back breathing down my neck. Mainly get in there, check it over, get anything dangerous like old black powder or dynamite out, and seal them up."

Mark looked into her eyes, and Beth was surprised by warmth in her belly that had nothing to do with the pizza. She'd been so caught up in trying to work the story angle that she hadn't realized just how cute he was. And his ring finger was bare.

She would have sworn she heard Clina chuckle deep inside her mind.

Chapter 8

"So, are we on to something here?" she said, and immediately blushed at how her words and thoughts matched up. He saved her by picking up his transparent plastic soda cup.

"Well, we're probably into a mess of regulations and red tape, to tell you the truth, but I think it's worth a try. To our future grave robbing adventures!"

"May they all rest in peace." Beth tapped his cup with hers.

She wished they had beer or wine instead of fountain soda, though too much booze would send her mind off in even more inappropriate directions. This bizarre situation Clina had dragged her into might turn out to have pretty damned good side benefits.

"I suppose we should get to know each other better if we're getting into such a macabre business together," Mark said, seeming to echo her thoughts. "Did you grow up in Hartstown? You don't quite sound like it."

"I grew up here, but my mother grew up in Chicago. I think her accent tempered dad's a bit, and we visited up there a lot. If we're talking accents, you don't sound like you're from here at all."

"That's where I'm sneaky," he said, raising one eyebrow with a crooked smile. "My parents are both natives. I was born here, but I grew up all over. Dad was in the Air Force until I was twenty. When he had long vacation time, we always came right back to Boun County."

"Odds are good we crossed paths some summer or another," Beth said, liking the sound of this more and more. Too many men she dated in college or on jobs refused to consider moving to such a small town. "Did the state station you here because of your family?"

"Wouldn't that be nice?" he said, shaking his head. Beth hoped her face didn't show how fast her heart sank. "We haven't had a full-time person down here for a couple of years. I've been reminding them I'd be perfect for the job for a few months. I'm only here for one more presentation, over in Abrams in the morning. Then it's back to Richmond."

"Oh," Beth said. She managed to keep from sighing. "I guess I misunderstood. I thought you… I thought these projects were starting up right away."

"Don't worry, I'll be back in a couple of weeks," Mark said, then it was his turn to blush. The ruddy color in his cheeks just made him look like he'd been hiking or running or something equally athletic. "Wow, did that sound overly confident. I meant we'll have preliminary funding in place by then. If I can give them a list of agreeable landowners, that might even speed things up."

"In the spirit of being overly confident, I'll do whatever I can to help." Beth hoped her recurrent blush was as attractive as his was.

By the time they shared a serving of banana pudding, agreeing it wasn't as good as their grandmothers made, Beth was more determined for herself than for Clina or the mysterious miner. Mark was the most interesting person she'd met in a long time, and by far the most interesting guy. Even if she had to convince a dozen cranky landowners to let them search for forgotten mines, every outcome she thought of was good.

"Looks like we're closing another place down," Mark said as he intercepted the check. "This was obviously a business dinner, so the Commonwealth should pay, right?"

"Obviously. You staying with family in town?"

"Yeah, for this trip," he said, rolling his eyes. "If I get something more permanent, that won't work out for long."

"I lasted about two weeks with my parents when I got back from college." They laughed together, and she turned to let Mark help with her coat. He put both hands on her shoulders for a second, more than long enough to get her full attention. He was smiling that gorgeous smile when she faced him. Beth gave him the card she'd dug out while he was paying for dinner. "Talk again when you're back in town?"

"I hope we'll talk before that," he said, handing her a business card. "My personal mobile is on the back."

"Then I'll speak to you soon."

Chapter 9

Beth gritted her teeth and slowed down for yet another gigantic rut in the overgrown gravel road. This narrow path through the thick brush and trees didn't have any kind of sign or number, only a faint blue trace on the thick book of county maps she'd checked out from the library. A few half-rotted trees, thankfully not quite blocking the way, made it clear no one else had been out here for a long while.

She'd also borrowed her brother's old four wheel drive work truck, knowing her sporty sedan wouldn't have a chance on these old farm and logging tracks. This was still a bigger challenge than she'd expected. Several well-maintained modern mining roads she'd already checked out were much easier to drive on, but they hadn't brought her any closer to that lonesome abandoned pit.

"Horse warns you of road trouble, not the other way round," Clina said.

"Yeah, I guess they do. This would take a month on a horse instead of a couple of days, too. Just let me know if you hear him getting closer."

After a good bit of contemplation about how quickly

she'd lose access to the archives if something went wrong, Beth had carefully packed up the funeral slide for these trips to make sure she could at least hear Clina. She was nowhere near as confident as her ghostly guide that she'd be able to hear the lost miner, much less figure out where he was.

"Who you wantin' me to listen out for? The miner or your new feller?"

Beth laughed out loud, then slipped the transmission back into four low for what looked like exposed boulders in a washed out section of the roadbed. She'd gotten used to conversations with a disembodied voice faster than she ever would have imagined.

"I hear from Mark often enough. You listen out for the miner."

The truth was not more than a few hours had passed without at least a text message from Mark since their pizza dinner a week ago. Beth knew she wasn't alone in looking forward to their long, flirty conversations more and more. Mark had flat out told her so the night before. His return in another week felt impossibly distant to her.

"I was wondering how we should approach this," Beth said. "Even after we find the right pit. Maybe I should have a false start or two instead of going right there. That would look a lot less suspicious."

"Here I was thinking you had smarts enough for this job. You forget this poor lost man has killed more folk than anyone's been able to count up? Like you told me, he ain't exactly limited himself to miners."

"I know, Clina. I just think it will seem too strange if I lead Mark right to a body on the first try."

"You mean if it seems like you did your research job, like you said you would?"

Beth rubbed her cheek in front of her left ear, trying to

get the annoying ringing to stop. Bobby's truck rattling was so much noisier than her car.

"I only said I was thinking about it," she said. "We have a little more time."

"We have time as long as this 'un don't try to pull more souls under the ground with him," Clina said, her voice sharp. "That'd be a ways past too late."

"I hear you, I hear—"

"Hush now! You're hearing the wrong thang!"

Chapter 10

Beth pulled over to the side of the narrow mud and gravel road, happy to avoid another giant rut right through the middle. She leaned forward and rubbed her face again, then gasped. That wasn't ringing in her ears. The tone was shifting, modulating from flat noise into a rising and falling song. Tears filled her eyes at the mournful sound even though she couldn't make out any words.

"Is that him?" Beth whispered, looking around.

She spotted a huge, modern coal storage tipple just over the ridgeline to the right, the squared-off, pale blue tower sharp against the bare trees and dark gray winter sky.

"That's who I been hearing all these long years. We're right near where all the troubles happen, ain't we?"

Beth pulled out her phone, amazed she got reception. Once she got a look at the real-time map, she understood why. This felt like a long-forgotten road in the middle of nowhere, but the middle of Hartstown was over the ridge to her left. If the old pit was close by here, it was no wonder things happened all over town as well as in the mines. Several of the giant ruts she'd driven across led to a good-sized creek on the other side of the road.

"We're close by the Mossy Rock #5 and #7 mines," Beth said, zooming the view out on the map. "Several disasters right here over the years, yeah. And town is just over the ridge. The cemetery is on the other side of this same mountain."

"No wonder I hear him so clear. Can you find out who owns these parts nowadays?

"I don't have to find out," Beth said, smiling despite the sorrowful cry echoing through her head. "This side belongs to Art Steffens, an attorney in town. He's in the habit of buying up land that's been mined or logged and planting hardwood trees. I can't imagine he'd object to cleaning up a dangerous old pit, especially on the state's tab."

"Well then, get your squeeze on that phone thang and get to work!"

Beth shook her head, driving forward and listening to the wailing getting louder. After about a quarter of a mile, the voice got weaker. She backed up until it was at an agonizing peak, so loud she could almost understand the words. She marked the spot on her map and on the phone, wondering if she'd be able to tolerate getting much closer. Her throat and chest felt like they were filling up with heavy, warm water, and more than a few tears spilled over.

"I still don't know about that, Clina. Hey, there's a gully, a gap in the trees, too. Might be a trail from a long time ago. I'd bet that's where we'll find our pit."

Beth heard a sigh, almost as loud as the singing.

"Wish you wouldn't waste my time and yours, tryin' to make a good impression on that feller. Seems to me he's impressed enough with you. If he's half as great as you tell me, I can't figure what either one of you's waiting for."

"Well, being in the same town instead of five hours apart would be an improvement," Beth said, trying to make mental notes of everything around her. "I've got three landowners on board already, so it won't take long. I'll go talk to Mr. Steffens right now."

Chapter 11

A FEW HOURS LATER, Beth grinned when she saw the number on her phone. The icy rain was too heavy to go outside, so she settled for closing the archives room door before she answered.

"Hey there, Mark."

"Hey Beth! I saw your email just now, fantastic! How'd you get so many people on board so fast?"

"I warned you," she said. "It's my irresistible charms. They let me dig into things no one else could because I make sure they enjoy every minute."

"I understand exactly how they feel," Mark said in a low voice. Beth smiled and closed her eyes, glad no one was there to see her. More than her face was warmer than usual. "Seriously, though, getting Art Steffens on board is huge. He probably owns several of those old pits, and the streams on his land feed right into the river. Well done."

"Thank you, sir," Beth said, wishing she could thank him in person. "So do you think this will help speed up your funding and starting work?"

"Well, that's why I'm calling, to warn you. When I told

the project manager how much land we'll have access to, he said we need to get started before everyone changes their minds. How's tomorrow sound?"

Beth laughed, hoping she'd covered the handset in time. She didn't want Mark or anyone else to know just how good that sounded, at least not until she was ready.

"I do appreciate the warning," she said, "but I'm afraid I can't get out of town fast enough to avoid you. What time do you get here?"

"Should be late afternoon if I can get enough things wrapped up here. Then we'll get started the next day. Did that killer investigator's mind of yours give you a hint of where we should dig in?"

Beth's smile faded, and she was glad Clina was busy singing work songs with what sounded like a herd of school kids. Maybe it was some kind of nagging guilt about insider information or something equally silly, but she was still worried about hitting the jackpot on their first try.

"I was thinking the Fleming place out near George's Gap would be a good place to start. I'd be more than happy to help you with directions and introductions, Mr. Hersch."

"That's something else I need to talk to you about, but I believe I'll keep it to myself until I see you in person."

"I'll look forward to your visit even more, then," Beth said. She flinched at an ear-splitting siren, one that had to be coming from the fire hall next door. An alarm had never gone off while she was so close. "Mark, I'm sorry, I have to go. Sounds like we have a fire or something here."

"Yeah, I hear that. Hope it's nothing bad. I'll give you a call tonight."

Chapter 12

BETH OPENED the door to general chaos, more than she'd ever seen in the town hall. Every office door was open, and several grim-faced people ran through in different directions. Tina was standing just inside the exit door, talking into her cell phone and crying. When she turned and saw Beth walking toward her, Tina met her in a tight hug.

"What's going on?" Beth said.

"There's been…" Tina stepped back, wiping at her face but barely able to talk. "A school bus went off the road heading out of town. Right into the river."

"Oh no," Beth whispered, her hand on her chest. "Are your boys okay?"

"No one knows yet. That's why they took the fire truck, in case the ambulances aren't enough. They won't let me go with them, even though I'm right here!"

Beth put her arm around Tina and looked at the fire hall's open door, and Beth knew they were thinking the same thing. A town this small didn't have a whole lot of rescue equipment or people trained to use it to begin with, certainly not for a bunch of kids caught in a nearly frozen river.

"Can I get you anything, Tina? I'm so sorry, but I don't know what to do."

"No one can do anything until we know more," Tina said, then seemed to pull herself together a little. "Listen, they're going to bring the kids who aren't hurt here to get warmed up and meet their parents. School was already out and we're closer. They need to keep the hospital clear for… the worst ones. It might get crazy."

"I'll wait and see if I can help," Beth said, wishing she could leave and avoid all of it. "Let me know, okay?"

Tina nodded just as her phone rang. Beth went back into the archives room, sick at her stomach. She didn't want to know the truth, but not knowing would drive her crazy. The voices in her head were singing old mountain dirges, further twisting her guts.

"Clina, I need to ask you something," Beth said, pulling the door around but not closing it. "Did we upset the miner? Being out there this morning?"

The singing stopped, but no one said anything.

"Come on, I need to know. Something awful just happened here. I can't send Mark or anyone else out to that pit unless—"

"I don't rightly know what makes him do what he does," Clina said in the softest voice Beth had heard from her. "His wailin' got louder after we was out there."

"I can't let Mark go walking in there," Beth whispered. "Once this miner gets a living person in that pit, he could bring the whole mountain down."

"I know you're afeared. I am myself. But if we don't do something now we got the chance to, he'll keep on forever. I got blood on my hands cause I only now got through to someone after decades trying. I done the best I could. Can you tolerate being among the living, the ones that's sufferin', and lettin' it go on?"

Beth sat forward with her elbows on the table, heels of her hands pressed against her eyes as if that could keep the tears inside. She could still smell Tina's flowery perfume on her clothes, still feel the panicky tightness of her hug. No one yet knew how bad this latest disaster was, but Beth was certain she knew what caused it.

Clina was right about not being able to live with letting it go on. But she didn't know if she could live with letting Mark be some kind of sacrifice, either.

"Is it even safe to bring his bones out of the mountain?" Beth said, shivering. "We have no idea how many people he's killed. Won't he get worse if he's not under tons of rock?"

"I'll not lie to you, Beth. You're the first to ever hear and try to help, and you deserve the truth even if it pains me to tell it. I don't rightly know if he'll get worse. All I know is how bad he's been up to now, and that he's cryin' out from bein' so lonesome. I can just hope he'll calm if he's here where I am and lots of others too."

"Can you help me, Clina? If I can manage to at least get close when Mark goes in there?"

"I swear to do everything in my power for you, and all the souls here with me swear the same."

Beth heard more voices, gathering up and getting louder, wordless affirmations that echoed and blended into one long hum.

Mmmm-hmmm. Mmmm-hmmm.

Chills covered her body, rising and falling with that internal reassurance. She had one last deep, strong fear about her own sanity, about trusting her life, Mark's and anyone else involved to ghosts, real or imagined.

"Well, everything you've told me checks out so far," Beth said, sitting back and wiping her face. "I don't have a lot of choice except to keep going."

She heard the first whimpers and cries of children

coming into the conference room behind her. Beth went out to help, dreading how bad it would be and hoping she could finally bring these long nightmares to an end.

Chapter 13

Beth paced in her living room, bare feet cold on the hardwood floor. She was too distracted and upset to do anything about that. Janie was curled up on the couch, her long red ears and black eyebrows shifting every time Beth passed by. Her heaviest hiking boots with thick socks tucked inside waited beside the front door. She planned to need those not long after Mark arrived.

Getting started tomorrow was no longer an option.

She glanced out for at least the hundredth time, wanting to see his state agency sedan turning up her driveway. Her brother's old truck was still out there. Beth hoped the abandoned road to the old pit wasn't impassable after the downpour of the last twenty-four hours.

She'd been a coward the night before and all day today when it came to telling Mark what was going on, sending him text messages instead of talking. Beth couldn't find the words, and she knew everyone in the state and the whole country would have heard by now.

Five out of the twenty-three children on that bus had drowned or given in to the awful cold after being caught in the water. Most of the rest were injured. It would have been a terrible tragedy anywhere in the country, but it was a disaster in this small town. With barely one hundred in the whole school, everyone knew who those lost kids were. Beth knew all of their families herself.

One of Tina's boys had a broken arm, the other a broken leg to go with many scrapes and bruises. She and her husband were like all the others who took their children home last night or could visit them at the hospital today. Relieved it hadn't been worse for their own family and struggling with sorrow and guilt for those not so lucky.

Beth's heart pounded when Janie barked at the sound of a car outside. She turned in time to see Mark getting out. A tiny part of her that wasn't heartbroken or terrified thought he was even more handsome than she remembered, his hair glinting in the sun coming through the last of the rain clouds. He waved, but he didn't smile. Beth went out to meet him.

"Beth, I'm so sorry about all this." She made it into his arms before she started crying. "Are you okay?"

"No, not really. I'm glad you're here."

He stroked her hair, and all Beth wanted to do was stay right there. Just go back inside, build a big fire in the woodstove, have dinner, and go to bed. Not to make love, though she'd been daydreaming about that more than a little until yesterday.

Now she wanted nothing more than to curl up safe and warm and go to sleep. She took a deep breath, then drew back to look into his eyes. Try as she might, she couldn't come up with a clever or calm way to explain anything, and she was out of time.

"Come on inside," she said. "I have some strange things to talk to you about."

After a few minutes of inspection and mutual approval

between Mark and Janie, he and Beth sat facing each other on the couch. Despite the droopy eyed hound head on his knee, the confused look on Mark's face didn't make starting this conversation any easier. Clina whispered inside Beth's head.

"You got everything you need to take care of this terrible thang. We'll be with you, and if he's half the man you think he is, he'll do all he can."

"I can't think of any other way to say it," Beth said. "I want to go out to one of those pits. Now, this afternoon."

"Hang on, we don't have everybody here yet," he said, his brow wrinkling.

"That's why we need to go now. I know they're not going to want me go in there, but I have to. I promise you I'll explain everything someday."

"Well, that was the thing I hadn't told you, Beth. My boss thinks we'll get the whole project off to a bigger start if we do your story as soon as we can, and he wants as much publicity as we can get. If we can get Mrs. Fleming to agree and everyone signs waivers, you can go inside with us right from the start. I'll have a photographer here tomorrow."

Beth smiled, surprised at how good a simple change in her facial muscles felt after the last several hours. If all the strangeness and sadness disappeared, she'd be delighted to have such an exciting story coming together. Almost as delightful as Mark's fingers twining through hers. His warmth lightened the sorrow of funeral songs she'd been hearing all day long in her head.

"That's great, thank you for setting that up," she said, squeezing his hand. "This is something a little different. I'll bring my camera. I can just about guarantee you we'll find the first set of remains tonight."

"What's going on? Have you heard something new?"

"You could say that. Did you bring enough gear for both of us?"

"Wait, I don't understand," Mark said. "The crew's on board with you going inside. Why does it have to be tonight?"

Chapter 14

Beth looked out the window, picking out the tipple they needed to go toward on the other side of town, the pale blue now vivid against the slate gray mountains, trying to find words that wouldn't make her sound crazier than she felt. She remembered one of the first things Clina said to her.

"This is going to sound strange." Beth looked into Mark's eyes, hoping the nervousness churning in her belly didn't show on her face. "Did you ever hear talk about a wise woman or a seer when you were visiting here? Anything like that?"

"My granddad had dreams no one could explain," Mark said without hesitation. "He always knew when something bad was coming, especially people dying. I don't think any of my family would have mentioned it anywhere else we lived, but every single one of us knew to heed his warnings. Never knew him to be wrong, either. He told me it came from his own grandfather, but I've heard of the same with women. Are you telling me you're a seer, Beth?"

Her heart and her breathing seemed to stop, but words found their way out anyway.

"Not exactly," she said. "At least I don't think so. I haven't seen anything, but I believe I'll be able to take you to a lost miner who needs to come up out of that mountain as soon as we can get to him. I can… I hear him. I know right where the pit is, at least where to park and start hiking."

Mark didn't frown, let go of her hand, or even raise his eyebrows.

"You believe this miner has something to do with what happened here yesterday?"

"I do," Beth said, trying to keep her trembling chin and voice from running away with the rest of her. "That and a lot of the other bad luck that lives and breathes in Hartstown."

He stared into her eyes for a few terribly long moments, then nodded.

"Fair enough. I brought respirators and gear for both of us, out in the car. Some axes and shovels, too, but the big equipment won't be here until tomorrow. Think we can get Mrs. Fleming's waivers handled first? Her son called me this morning. Sounded like he's going to want to argue for a while before he'll get out of the way and let her sign."

"You're right about her son, but that's the best part," Beth said, letting out a breath she didn't remember holding. "This mine is on Art Steffen's land. His office is right across from the town hall, and he's been asking me nonstop when we can get started."

Mark smiled, and Beth's eyes filled with tears. These weren't the hot, painful tears she'd shed too many of since yesterday and most of the night, the ones she'd been trying to fight back all day. These were tears of relief from the deepest part of her.

"I've got the paperwork with me, too," Mark said. "We'll take care of that on the way."

Chapter 15

Beth parked the truck and rotated her shoulders, trying to work out the tense knots from the trip. She'd had serious doubts more than once. The creek was much higher than before, and the ruts all had deep standing water. Her first trip out gave her a good idea which parts to aim for, but not one part of the drive had been easy.

"Good driving, Beth," Mark said. "I never would have made it. Too much city living. Here, let me."

She turned toward the driver's side window, and he dug his strong fingers into the worst spots. Good as it felt, Beth was staring through a long crack in the glass directly at the gap in the bigger oak and maple trees. Between that and the wailing, she'd never be able to relax. The lost miner was far louder than he'd been just a couple of days ago.

"That's a huge help, thank you," she said, facing Mark. "Listen, we're going to have to be careful here. This guy's been trying to pull people down there with him for a long time."

He looked out the window past her, then focused on

Beth. She was afraid she'd gone too far, said one too many crazy things.

"We'll do our best. Mr. Steffens knows where we are, and I sent a text message to a couple of the crew on the way. I didn't tell them much, just that I got here early so we're going to check it out. If we can get to him, what are we supposed to do?"

"Remember the mass grave I told you about?" Beth said. "I hope if we put him in there he'll rest easier."

"Makes sense to me," he said. "Let's see what we can do."

Before she could talk herself out of it, Beth put both hands behind his neck and pulled him into a kiss. In that heat and touch, she forgot everything. Her sadness, her fears, her uncertainty that they should be out there at all. Beth held on to the one thing she did know. Her lips and Mark's were meant to be together.

"Now I'm about a thousand times more determined to get back out of there," Mark said, his cheeks flushed and his breathing faster. "Hear anything that might help us?"

Beth took the chance to catch her own breath as she grabbed her backpack from behind the seat. She pulled out Clina's glass negative and unwrapped it.

"Whatever it is seems to be linked to her," she said, touching Clina's white hat. "She's the one I'm hearing. I thought I was crazy at first, but I checked out a bunch of things she told me over at the courthouse. Every word was true."

Mark took the slide by the plastic-covered edges and held it up to the sun, still up but moving lower.

"How old is this? Do you know who—"

He touched the image and nearly dropped the glass, catching it against his thighs. He turned to Beth, tears in his eyes.

"The crying voice. Is that what you hear?"

Beth's jaw dropped, and she heard Clina and a few other people laugh.

"That's who we're here for," she said. "Do you hear anyone else? A woman?"

"No," Mark said slowly, holding the slide up again. "Just a man. I don't think I could stand to hear anyone else. Do you hear others?"

"I do," Beth said. "She's the main one, and she promised to help us as much as she can. I'll do my best to explain it all once we're out of here."

Mark leaned forward and kissed Beth again, humming deep in his throat. He put the slide carefully on the seat between them.

"We better go before I lose my nerve," he said. "Or before it gets too much later. It won't matter while we're inside, but I can't imagine the drive out will be easier in the dark. Sounds to me like we're heading up that little gap there."

"The road gets a little clearer from here," she said, "but the sooner the better. I can't tell you how glad I am you hear him, too."

"You and me both." Mark winked and opened his door. "I like you too much to think you were losing it just yet."

"Okay, Clina," Beth said under her breath when he closed the door. "We're here. We could use all the help you can send us."

"I got a big crowd gathered up waitin' for you. Some here think they knew the man in life. One even knew your feller, there, when he was a tiny boy. We'll do every little thang we can. Might manage some big thangs, too."

Chapter 16

THEY BOTH WORE OLD JEANS, heavy boots, and thick flannel shirts. Even with temperatures in the mid-forties, they'd be plenty warm hiking up the mountain. Mark was waiting beside the truck with knee and elbow pads, a bright yellow helmet with a light on the front, clear plastic goggles, and a dark blue respirator. Instead of the full face device she'd feared, it was only big enough to fit over her nose and mouth. There were three round fan-like openings at the bottom, and he held it by two straps.

"This one isn't heavy duty enough for hours in an active mine," he said. "But it should be fine for what we need. The full crew will have bigger gear with air tanks and all."

"I'd rather not have anything bigger than this," Beth said. "I don't think I could breathe in one of the whole face ones."

They slipped everything into her pack, and Mark handed her a short black metal shovel. He clipped an old but well cared for machete to his belt and grabbed a pickaxe, pointed on one end and flat on the other.

"You'll do just fine," he said. "It took me a while, but I

finally got used to it. Ready to see if we can help this poor guy?"

Beth's nerves, on edge since she'd first seen Tina crying the day before, threatened to close her throat. Neither of them had any idea what they were walking into.

"Mark, he's killed a lot of people over the years. He probably had something to do with what happened yesterday."

"Sounds like more than enough reason to see what we can do to get him out of here," he said, taking her hand. "I don't think I've heard a more lonesome sound in my whole life. I know company makes me feel a whole lot better."

After about ten minutes of hiking up the muddy gully with several stops to clear the tangled undergrowth, Beth stopped. The narrow path ended ahead of them with a stand of huge oaks and poplar trees easily a hundred years old. They stood on a small level patch with higher ground close by on both sides, but there was another gap to the right. Only a few scrubby trees and low brush grew there, and Beth was sure she saw a darker area behind them.

"Do you hear it stronger over there?" she said, pointing.

Mark turned his head that way and nodded.

"Much stronger. Looks like an opening, too. I've never seen this on any map of old mines. Could be a house coal pit. If we looked around a bit more, I imagine we'd find what's left of his homestead."

Once they cut and pulled the brush away and moved a fallen tree limb, they found a gap between the rocks almost as tall as Beth. They could easily pass through one at a time. Scattered black bits of coal stood out along the dark gray rock underfoot. The singing was nearly a scream in her mind.

"Is this it, Clina?" Beth said under her breath.

"You found the very place. We're gonna do what we can, but you best be careful there, you and your feller."

She watched Mark wipe sweat from his face, then swing

his pack to the ground. He smiled at her, that ruddy flush in his cheeks again, looking more excited than afraid.

"We will."

After helping her with the gear and making sure the respirator was fitted properly, Mark settled it down around her neck.

"We'll see what it's like in there," he said. "These house mines usually aren't all that deep. If we stir up too much dust, we'll be ready. Let me know if you hear anything strange, all right?"

"Yeah, you too," Beth said. "Clina thinks it was a rock fall, so we need to keep an eye on the roof."

They turned on their lights and headed into the cave. The floor was fairly smooth, with gouges in the rock that looked like they were cleared long ago. Coal or dust had settled on every surface. After the fresh, humid air outside, Beth wrinkled her nose at the dry, musty smell. She was starting to worry about smelling a man dead for at least a hundred years until she saw piles of leaves and sticks on the floor. Something small had nested here a long time ago.

"You don't think this is big enough for a bear to be sleeping in, do you?" Mark said, stopping in front of her.

"The stink would be a lot stronger than this. Black bears smell like garbage dumps. I think that's the least of our worries."

After about ten feet, they saw the start of the coal seam on the left wall. It was narrow at first, just a few inches around Beth's shoulder height, then dug out when it got a little thicker further on. The gouged out shelf got thicker and higher until it blended into the gray rock above them.

Beth felt like all the bones in her body were vibrating with the keening that seemed to be all around them. She couldn't quite catch the words the group in her head was singing, but the tune sounded a lot like "Barbara Allen." She couldn't imagine how such tragic lyrics could help. Mark stopped again, pulling a much brighter flashlight off his belt.

"We've got to be close judging by his cry alone," he said, his voice not much more than a whisper.

He moved the light slowly along the roof, stopping when the fairly smooth black and grey expanse gave way to a huge jagged hole. As he lowered the beam toward the floor, it turned from clean white to dingy gray. The dust and dirt came from above.

"Get your mask on, Beth."

Chapter 17

Mark pulled his mask up with his free hand, then took a
step backward. Beth moved with him. Before she could say a
word, several large pieces of coal and rock fell, the noise deafening in the tiny cave. A chunk of limestone easily two feet
wide and three feet long landed where he'd just been
standing.

"Safe bet he knows we're here," Beth said, her voice
muffled by the respirator. "You okay?"

"I'm good. I think we found our man."

She followed the light and saw pale white through the
shifting dust. The skull and arms were unmistakable, as were
the long leg bones. The torso was hidden by a pile of rocks,
none of them as big as the one that had just missed Mark.

They'd obviously been big enough.

The man's arms and fingers had been stretched out
toward the entrance for decades, desperate to escape his
hellish trap. Only his voice and malevolent spirit had ever
made it.

"Clina?" Beth said, her stomach roiling at the thought of
anyone trapped in a black hole like this.

"You done made it to the right spot." Voices still sang in the background, but Beth heard Clina loud and clear. The miner's mournful singing had turned to screaming. "He's not happy 'bout you bein' there."

"Can you help us?" Beth said. "We can't get him out if he's going to drop rocks on our heads."

Mark turned to watch her, eyebrows raised, but he didn't say a word.

"Grab on to your feller so maybe he can hear me." Beth took Mark's gritty hand, and they both jumped when Clina shouted. "Now listen here! These folks mean to help you! I don't plan to spend another hunnerd years tryin' to get you away from there. Stop actin' a fool and let them take you out!"

"Clina?" Mark whispered. Beth nodded. "Is it safe now?"

"I have no earthly idea," she said. "He still sounds angry to me."

"He's right full of piss," Clina said. "We got him pushed back a mite. I feel like if we hold tight to him, kindly surround him, he might understand."

"I don't feel reassured," Beth said. "Can we do anything to help?"

"Besides carryin' him outta there? Try doing the same. Think on holdin' him wrapped up like in a quilt. I make no promise, but I hope that helps him to feel safe."

"Did you hear that, Mark?"

"Try to wrap him up in a mental quilt, and no promises," he said, and Beth saw the smile in his eyes above the mask. "I was thinking more of putting him in a backpack, but I'm glad to do whatever works."

They stepped forward over the huge rock, Mark's flashlight still aimed at the roof. The dust was starting to settle, but both left the respirators on. When they got close enough, Beth saw more of what happened. The man's spine was damaged. Two of the vertebrae in the middle of his ribs were compressed in a strange way.

"I'm sorry I don't know your name, sir," Mark said, focusing his attention and the light on the bones. "We're here to bring you out and give you a good burial. Will you let us do that?"

"You heed that feller now," Clina said. Beth had let go of Mark's hand, and he gave no sign of hearing. "These good people aim to help you."

Mark shrugged his pack off and knelt beside the skull, still glancing uneasily at the roof. The voices with Clina rose as the miner's got quieter. A huge crowd singing "Amazing Grace," Clina speaking the words right before the group answered, was louder than his low moan.

"We do want to help you," Beth said, joining Mark on the rubble strewn floor. "We can take you to a place where you won't be so lonesome."

Beth heard the whispery fracture just as Mark reached toward the skull, a split second before Clina and everyone with her shouted in her mind.

"Mark!"

Chapter 18

Beth launched herself sideways onto her hip, shoving Mark away, wincing when his helmet smacked against the wall. Before she could move, more rock dropped from the roof. A thick chunk of coal landed on her upper arm, knocking her flat. The pain was immediate and huge. Beth screamed, the miner's voice shrieking an answer.

"What happened?" Mark shook his head, his words slow. He sat up and found her with his headlight. "Beth!"

"I think it's just my arm," she said, her voice tight.

She gritted her teeth when he helped her sit up. She'd have bruises from the rest of the rocks, but Beth was sure the bone was broken.

"That's it, we have to get out of here," Mark said. "Can you stand?"

"No, wait," Beth said. "This is why we came in here. I can't let this go on."

Beth looked at the bones when she spoke, doing everything she could to direct the words toward the lost miner. Her arm was throbbing every time she breathed, but she couldn't just walk away.

"It doesn't matter why. Not anymore." Mark picked up his pack and the flashlight before he reached for her good arm. "This roof is unstable. We can try again with the full crew."

"No!" Beth shouted. Mark drew back, and she fought down her urge to apologize. That wouldn't get her anywhere right now, and it could get both of them and who knew who else killed. "Clina, I need you all to help me now. We have to make him understand."

The voices in her head stopped, leaving her inner ears ringing in the silence. The miner's voice whispered like the wind on a bitter night.

"Mark, help me," Beth said. "I need to stand up so we can face him together."

He held her with one arm around her waist and the other supporting her good hand, but Beth cried out more than once before she was on her feet. She gripped Mark's hand and looked at the skull now covered with dirt.

"Listen to me," Beth said. Clina and many others repeated her words in a dozen accents. "I know you're alone and afraid. We're the first people in a hundred years who can help you. We can take you out of here right now. If you try to hurt us again, we'll leave you here. We'll come back tomorrow and blow this place up. You'll be alone for all eternity."

She paused, and Clina spoke into the silence, the echoes a few seconds behind.

"Not a one of us'll speak to you no more. We done all we can to tend to you, but you tried to hurt my friends. The wall of cold and empty I will build up around you will make your deep hell seem like a fairy land o' milk and honey."

The air around them seemed to compress, the dust frozen in place. Another huge pile of rocks tumbled down from the roof a few feet away. Mark drew Beth back with him.

"Beth, please, we have to get out of here."

"There are a hundred people underground, in the mine just across the creek. Some of them haven't buried their kids yet. Not even the roads are safe anymore. We have to get him out of here."

Beth stepped forward into the shifting dust.

"We have a place ready for you. You'll be with a bunch of other people. Clina and her friends will make sure you're safe. Please don't make us leave you here alone now that we finally found you."

"I know you hear me right now," Clina said, her voice gentle. "Let them take you out of there, and we'll make sure you're never lonesome again."

The whispery voice in Beth's head grew louder until she realized the air in the cave was actually moving. She took a step back despite her determination.

"It's moving out," Mark said, squeezing her hand. "The air's clearing out."

He swung the flashlight around, and the beam shone cleaner by the second. Before Beth could count to ten, not even normal cave dust was visible. She let go of Mark's hand and lowered her respirator.

"I think we got hold of him for now," Clina said. "Don't know how long we can keep him, so best get to movin'."

"Thank you," Beth said, to the miner, Clina, and Mark. This time her words were echoed in many languages. Italian, German, French, and several she didn't recognize. "We want to take your bones from this place and bury you with a great group. They'll welcome you home."

"We surely will," Clina said, and again voices from different parts of the world joined in.

"I'm a son of these mountains just like this woman is a daughter," Mark said. "I know the pain of being far off from home. Let us do what we can to calm your soul."

Chapter 19

Mark knelt again, holding a trembling hand over the skull for a few seconds before he touched it. For the first time since Beth first heard it, the miner's voice fell silent. Mark gently picked up the skull and slipped it into his pack. Beth squatted as carefully as she could and picked up the left upper arm bone, then the right. Within a few minutes, they'd shifted the original rock fall aside and gathered up everything they could see.

"Thank you for letting us help you," Beth said, her voice trembling from worsening pain in her arm. Sweat cut tracks through the grime on her face. "We'll bring you out of here, and bury you as soon as we possibly can."

"I know just the place for the night," Mark said. "Right beside my grandfather. They might have a lot to talk about. Come on, we need to get you to the hospital."

He pulled off his flannel shirt and tied it into a makeshift sling. Her arm still hurt, but the relief was dramatic.

"Sounds great to me," she said, kissing his cheek. "As long as we get our friend here settled first."

"I have an idea of the answer, but is there any point arguing with you?"

"None at all."

The soft breeze continued as they walked back out of the cave, clearing the dust and dirt in front of them. As soon as they stepped outside, a rumble built from deep within the pit. Beth heard rock falling in a wave, moving toward them in slow motion. Mark pulled his respirator on again and helped Beth with hers just as a thick plume of dust burst outward.

Within a few seconds, the air was still. Any sense of movement, of life, inside the abandoned pit ceased to exist. The brush and trees on the outside were coated an eerie pale gray all around them. Mark held his light out far enough to light up the entrance. Neither of them could have fit back through the rocks piled up there.

Beth leaned against a huge oak, trying to slow her breathing. She appreciated the humid but much colder air more than she would have ever imagined. The orange light was fading all around them.

By the time they made it back to the truck, Beth leaning on the shovel or Mark's back for the worst parts, she was trembling with cold and agony. When he loaded everything into the bed of the truck except his own pack, she saw gooseflesh rippling his bare arms. She tried to reach her right pocket, but it hurt too much.

"Can you get the keys, Mark? The road's a lot better from here on out. I don't think I can manage driving."

"Of course. Come on, I'll help you up."

Once they were settled in the truck with the engine started, the pack on the floor between them, Beth remembered the negative on the seat.

"Mark," she whispered. "Look."

The glass was shattered into dozens of pieces, but none of

them had moved. The image was still perfectly aligned and clear.

"Our miner's last victim," Mark said, his eyes wide. "Can you still hear Clina?"

"I hear them singing. 'Auld Lang Syne' of all things. It's kind of perfect."

"It is," he said, resting his hand on her knee. "I just realized we forgot to get any pictures."

Beth laughed hard enough to jar her arm, but she barely felt it. She covered his hand with hers.

"We'll do better next time. Assuming Clina will help us out again."

Mark leaned closer to the pieces of glass and picked up one of the larger ones. He held Clina's face and her big white hat in his fingers.

"I have a feeling she will."

Chapter 20

THE NEXT AFTERNOON, Mark and Beth returned to the town cemetery half an hour before the groundskeeper was supposed to meet them. She'd been on the phone most of the morning getting this impromptu burial arranged, wanting to be certain nothing would interfere with the heartbreaking funerals taking place over the next few days. Beth's right arm was in a thick cast from right below her shoulder to just past her bent elbow. At least the break was clean.

"Want to stay here and I'll get him?" Mark said, parking his blue sedan.

"I'll go with you."

She did let him manage the tricky business of opening the door.

The Hersch family plots were in the shaded, hilly part of the cemetery, some of the oldest ones still left. Three rows back from the road stood an average light gray stone set right into the hillside. Mark leaned around and picked up his backpack, undisturbed from the night before.

"Walton Mark Hersch," Beth said, her fingers tracing the engraved words. "Were you named after him?"

"Sure was," he said. "No matter what my sister or cousins say, I was his favorite. Can you still hear anything?"

Beth reached into her jacket pocket to touch the fragment of glass, the sharp edges wrapped with plastic. While they'd waited at the hospital, Mark had told her about an artist who could coat the edges in metal and seal the whole thing to protect it. She'd already decided to let him do just that. Copper would suit Clina perfectly.

"Still right here, not that you need the likes of me," Clina said, and Beth was sure she was smiling. "You done good, Beth, you and that man of yours. His granddaddy is right proud a both of you. Says that one you rescued chattered a blue streak at him all night long. Couldn't understand a word, but he was glad to listen. I reckon we'll puzzle it out."

The voices in the background sounded like some kind of party gathering, maybe an old church social. At least a couple of fiddles were tuning up.

"She's there," Beth said. "She says your grandfather is proud. And that we did good."

"We did." Mark smiled and put his arm around her waist, careful not to touch her cast. "I'm glad Papaw approves. Do we know much about our miner yet?"

Beth heard a deep voice, one she'd only heard crying or screaming before. She couldn't make out the language, but he sounded calm. And happy.

"Not yet," she said. "The senior Mr. Hersch said he was a bit hard to understand, but they're working on it."

"Good. Let's get him laid him to rest."

The state photographer and groundskeeper were waiting by the low black crypt marking the mass grave. In the end, the procedure was remarkably simple. The burly, bearded man worked the edge of a long piece of iron under the marble slab and shifted it several inches to the side. A metal chute led down into darkness.

Mark laid out white cotton flannel they'd found in Beth's sewing stash. The photographer clicked away while they lined up the bones on the fabric, then rolled it into a neat bundle.

"May your rest be easy," Mark said, holding the bundle over the chute.

"And your troubles be few," Beth said.

"We welcome you home with open arms," Clina said, and a chorus raised up with her.

The miner was singing again, but this time it was the sound of pure joy.

Mark let the fabric slide down into the grave. Beth stepped forward with a smaller bundle he'd helped her make that morning, slipping it after the bones of the lost miner. The glass made a barely audible jangle at the bottom.

"Thank you, Clina Jane," she said. "I hope to hear from you again."

"You best count on it, Beth. Likely be busy for a spell though. Gotta put your miner to work. We need all the help we can get makin' these little young'uns welcome."

ABOUT KARI

The daughter, granddaughter, and great-granddaughter of coal miners, Kari Kilgore's wanderlust and imagination lead her all over the world on grand adventures. Her heart and family bring her home to her native Appalachian Mountains of Virginia. From that solid base, she and her husband Jason A. Adams bring those adventures to life in fiction.

Kari writes science fiction, fantasy, and horror, and she's happiest when she scares herself. She lives at the end of a long dirt road in the middle of the woods with Jason, various house critters, and wildlife they're better off not knowing more about.

The Confidential Adventure Club

For Kari's exclusive free After The End stories and deleted scenes, discounts, early pre-sale releases, adorable pet photos, and a whole lot more not available anywhere else, visit The Confidential Adventure Club at www.smarturl.it/c-a-club.

Hope to see you there!

www.karikilgore.com
www.spiralpublishing.net

ALSO BY KARI KILGORE

I hope you enjoyed reading *Songs in the Mountain* as much as I enjoyed writing it. For more with Beth, Mark, and Clina, check out *Secrets in the Land* at www.karikilgore.com.

The Confidential Adventure Club

Want more fiction from Kari, including stories, discounts, and box sets not available anywhere else? Want to hear about locations, research, and other cool things that inspired this story and beyond? All that and adorable pet photos, too?

Join The Confidential Adventure Club and get a thank you gift of a free short story and a whole lot more at www.smarturl.it/c-a-club.

Hope to see you there!

Novels:

Until Death

The Dream Thief

Dreaming the Storm: Book One of the Storms of Future Past Series

Joining the Storm: Book Two of the Storms of Future Past Series

Fighting the Storm: Book Four of the Storms of Future Past Series

Novellas:

Legacy of the Land

Restricted Species

The Becalmed

In the Pines

Into the Storm: Book Three of the Storms of Future Past Series

Secrets in the Land: Book Two of the Voices through Time Series

Short Stories:

Renovations

Intentions

The Garbage Belt

The Seeds of Love

Wicked Bone

The Sound of Murder

Terminalia

Little Five: A Terminalia Story

Reflections

The Last Dragonkeeper

The Earworms

Collections:

Fantastic Women: A Dark Fantasy Novella Trio

Fantastic Shorts: Volume 1 - A Fantasy Short Story Collection

Storms of Future Past Books One through Four

Near Future Forward (with Jason A. Adams)

"Kari Kilgore is an author to watch—her lyrical voice a siren song; her insight, conjured voodoo."

—Richard Thomas, author of *Breaker* and *Tribulations*